The NatureTrail Book of TREES & LEAVES

Ingrid Selberg

Identifying Trees with this Book

This book is about the common trees you can see. It tells you about the different parts of a tree and how they work. When you see a tree and you want to know its name, or more about it, use the book as follows:

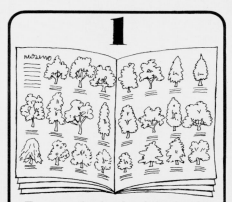

1

Turn to the back of the book (pages 28-31) and look it up in the section called **Common Trees to Spot**. If you can't see a picture of it there . . .

2

. . . turn to the page in the book which deals with **the part of the tree** which you are looking at. For example, pages 16-17 tell you about fruits and seeds.

Always make careful notes about the trees you see so that you can identify them later.

USBORNE

First published in 1977 by
Usborne Publishing Ltd,
20 Garrick Street,
London WC2

Text and Artwork © 1977 by
Usborne Publishing Ltd.

Silver Birch

Written by
Ingrid Selberg

Consultant Editor
E. H. M. Harris, B.Sc., Dip.For.
F.I.For., Director of the Royal
Forestry Society

Designed by
Sally Burrough

Illustrated by
John Barber, Christine Darter,
John Francis, Victoria Gordon,
Tim Hayward, Christine Howes
Malcolm McGregor, Barbara
Nicholson.

Printed in Belgium

The name Usborne and the device are
Trade Marks of Usborne Publishing Ltd.

Norway Maple

Red Horse Chestnut

Apples

The NatureTrail Book of
TREES & LEAVES

About This Book

Trees are around you everywhere. This book tells you about trees and how to study them. It shows you the different parts of a tree, how they work and how they can help you to identify the tree. It tells the whole story of a tree, from when it sprouts from a seed to when it dies or is cut down for timber. The book also includes special tips on how to collect information and specimens from trees. If you want to identify a tree, follow the instructions on page 1.

Contents

How to Identify Trees 4
How a Tree Grows 6
What to Look for on a Tree
  Leaves 8
  Winter Buds 10
  Shape 12
  Bark 13
  Flowers 14
  Fruits and Seeds 16
Grow Your Own Seedling 18

Forestry 19
Annual Rings 20
Wood 21
Pests and Fungi 22
Injuries 23
Woodland Life 24
Making a Tree Survey 26
Common Trees to Spot
  Conifers 28
  Broadleaved Trees 29
Index, Books to Read,
  Clubs and Societies 32

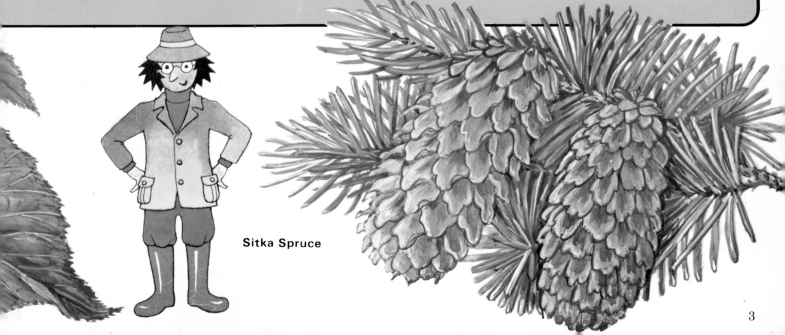

Sitka Spruce

How to Identify Trees

When you want to identify a tree, the first things to look at are its leaves. But there are some trees whose leaves are very similar – for example, a Lombardy Poplar leaf could be confused with a Birch leaf. So always use at least one other feature, such as the flowers or bark, to help you identify a tree. (See pictures below.)

Trees can be divided into three groups: broadleaved, coniferous, and palm trees (see right). Try to decide to which group your tree belongs.

There is something to help you identify trees in every season. In spring and summer, look at the leaves and flowers. In autumn, many trees bear fruits which are good clues for identification. Winter is the best time to study buds, twigs, bark and tree shapes.

You do not need to go into a forest to find trees. Look at the many different kinds that grow in gardens, roads and in parks. Sometimes you can find rare trees in gardens.

Broadleaved Trees

Lime (winter)

Oak (summer)

Beech (spring)

Beech leaf and flower

Japanese Maple (autumn)

Most broadleaved trees have wide, flat leaves which they drop in winter. Some broadleaved trees, however, such as Holly, Laurel, Holm Oak and Box, are evergreen and keep their leaves in winter.

Broadleaved trees have seeds that are enclosed in fruits. The timber of broadleaved trees is called hardwood, because it is usually harder than the wood of most conifers, or softwood trees.

Tree or Shrub?

Tree

Shrub

6 m

Trees are plants that can grow to over 6 m high on a single woody stem. Shrubs are generally smaller, and have several stems. See page 27 for how to measure trees.

What to Look for

Leaves

Yew (Conifer)

Oak (Broadleaf)

Beech (Broadleaf)

The leaves will give you the biggest clue to the identity of the tree, but look at other parts of the tree as well. There is a guide to leaves on page 8.

Shape and Bark

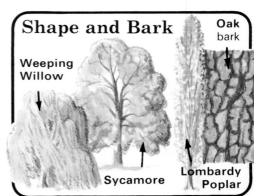

Oak bark

Weeping Willow

Sycamore

Lombardy Poplar

The overall shape of the tree, and of its top, or crown, are also good clues. Some trees can be recognized just by looking at their bark. See pages 12–13.

Conifers

Norway Spruce

Palms

Leaf

Scots Pine

Cone and needles

European Larch (in winter)

European Larch (in summer)

Canary Palm

Most conifers have narrow, needle-like or scaly leaves, and are evergreen. The Larch is one conifer that is not evergreen. Conifer fruits are usually woody cones, but some conifers, like the Yew, have berry-like fruits. The overall shape of conifers is more regular than that of most broadleaved trees.

Palms have trunks without branches that look like giant stalks. The leaves grow at the top of the tree. Unlike other trees, the Palm grows taller, without getting thicker.

Winter Buds

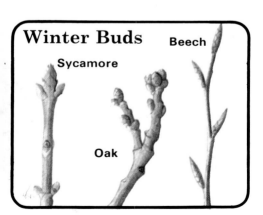

Sycamore

Beech

Oak

In winter, when there are no leaves to look at, you can still identify some trees from their buds, bark and shape. See page 11 for a guide to bud shapes.

Flowers

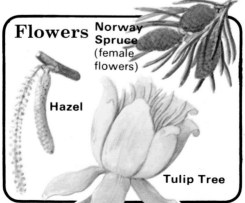

Norway Spruce (female flowers)

Hazel

Tulip Tree

In certain seasons trees have flowers which can help you to recognize the tree. But some trees do not flower every year. See pages 14–15.

Fruits and Seeds

Horse Chestnut fruit

Scots Pine cone

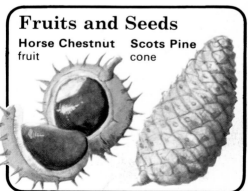

All trees have fruits bearing seeds which may grow into new trees. This Horse Chestnut 'conker' and pine cone are both fruits. See pages 16–17.

How a Tree Grows

This is the life story of a Sycamore, but all trees grow in a similar way. Although there are many different kinds of trees, they all sprout from seeds, grow larger, flower, form fruits and shed seeds.

There are many stages of a tree's life story that you can study. You can watch it sprout from a seed and then chart its growth. You can count the girdle scars on a young tree to find out how old it is.

Older trees all have flowers and fruits at some time in most years, although they may be hard to see on some trees. They are not all as large as the Horse Chestnut's flowers or the fruit of the Apple tree. Not all fruits ripen in autumn. Some appear in early summer and even in spring.

An important part of a tree that you do not see is the roots. If you find an overturned tree, look at the roots and try to measure them. Look also at logs and tree stumps for the layers of wood and bark. They can tell you the age of the tree and its rate of growth.

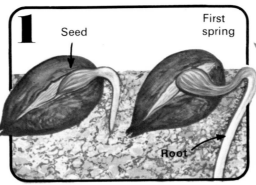

1 Seed / First spring / Root

The tree starts growing in spring from a seed which has been lying in the soil all winter. Now, with the help of the food stored inside it, the seed sends down a root into the soil to suck up water and minerals.

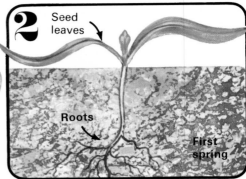

2 Seed leaves / Roots / First spring

Then the seed sends up a shoot which pokes above the ground and into the light. Two fleshy seed leaves open up with a small bud between them. These leaves are not the same shape as the tree's ordinary leaves will be.

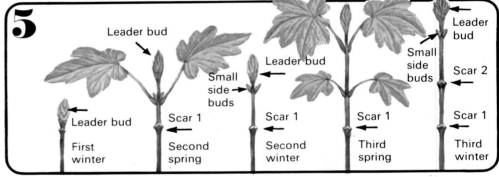

5 Leader bud / Small side buds / Leader bud / Scar 2 / Leader bud / Scar 1 / Leader bud / First winter / Scar 1 / Second spring / Scar 1 / Second winter / Scar 1 / Third spring / Scar 1 / Third winter

The following spring, the bud opens and a new shoot grows, with leaves at the tip. In autumn, they drop off. The next year, the same thing happens, and each year when the leaves fall off, they leave a girdle scar on the stem. Buds on the sides of the stem also grow shoots in the summer. But they do not grow as fast as the leader shoot at the top of the tree. Each year the tree grows taller, and the roots grow deeper.

8 Pollen on the flowers

When the tree is about twelve years old, it grows flowers on its branches in the spring. Bees, searching for nectar, visit the flowers and some of the pollen from the flowers sticks on to their hairy bodies.

9 Fruits

When the bees visit other Sycamore flowers, some of the pollen on their bodies rubs off on to the female parts of the flowers. When the male (pollen) and female parts are joined, the flowers are fertilized and become fruits.

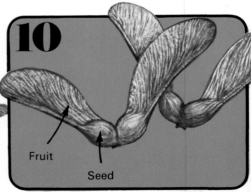

10 Fruit / Seed

Later that year, the fruits fall off the tree, spinning like tiny helicopters, carrying the seeds away from the parent tree. The wings rot on the ground, and the seeds are ready to grow the following spring.

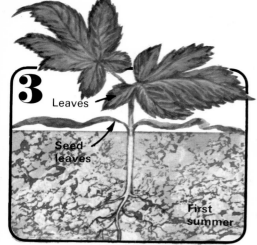

3 Leaves

Seed leaves

First summer

The seed leaves have stored food in them to help the tree grow. Soon the bud opens, and the first pair of ordinary leaves appears. The seed leaves then drop off. The roots grow longer.

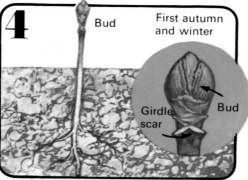

4 Bud

First autumn and winter

Girdle scar

Bud

In the autumn, all the leaves change colour and drop off, leaving a "girdle scar" around the stem where they were attached, and a bud at the end of the shoot. The bud does not grow during the winter.

Holly leaf

Many broadleaved trees are deciduous, which means that they lose their leaves in autumn. They do this because their leaves cannot work properly in cold weather, and there is not enough sunlight in winter for the leaves to make food for the tree.

Most conifers are called evergreens because they keep their leaves throughout the winter. Their needles are tougher than most broadleaves, and they can keep making food even in the dark of winter.

A few broadleaved trees, such as Holly, are also evergreen. Like conifer needles, their leaves have a waxy coating which helps them survive the winter.

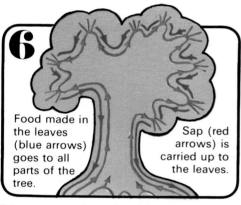

6

Food made in the leaves (blue arrows) goes to all parts of the tree.

Sap (red arrows) is carried up to the leaves.

The tree makes food for itself in its leaves, which contain a green chemical called chlorophyll. In sunlight, the chlorophyll can change air, water and minerals brought up from the soil into food for the tree.

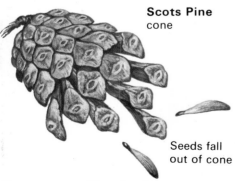

Scots Pine cone

Seeds fall out of cone

Some trees, like the Scots Pine, have fruits called cones, which stay on the tree, but open up to let the seeds fall out by themselves. When the cones are old and dried up, they usually fall off the tree too.

7

1
Bark is the outer layer which protects the tree from sun, rain and fungi which might attack it.

2
Tubes. Just inside the bark are tubes which carry food down from the leaves to all parts of the tree including the roots.

3
Cambium. This layer is so thin that you can hardly see it. Its job is to make a new layer of sapwood each year. This makes the trunk thicker and stronger.

4
Sapwood. This layer also has tiny tubes in it which carry the sap (water and minerals) to all parts of the tree from the roots. Each year a new "ring" of this wood is made by the cambium.

5
Heartwood. This is old sapwood which is dead and has become very hard. It makes the tree strong and rigid.

6
Rays. In a cross-section of a log you can see pale lines. These are called rays and they carry food sideways.

Each year the tree bears more branches. The stem thickens to hold them up, and the roots grow deeper and wider. The stem adds a new layer of wood. This picture shows you the inside of the stem, or trunk, and its different parts.

Leaves

The first thing that most people notice about a tree is its leaves. A big Oak tree has more than 250,000 leaves and a conifer may have many millions of needles.

The leaves fan out to the sunlight, and with the green chlorophyll inside them, they make food for the tree. They take in gases from the air and give out water vapour through tiny holes. Once the food is made, it is carried through veins to other parts of the leaf. The veins also strengthen the leaf like a skeleton.

The leaf stem brings water from the twig and also helps the leaf to move into the light. It is tough so that the leaf does not break off in strong winds.

Although the leaves of conifers and broadleaved trees look different, they both do the same work. Most conifer leaves can survive the winter, but broadleaves fall off in the autumn. Conifers also lose their leaves, but not all at once. A pine needle stays on a tree for about three to five years.

Conifer Leaves

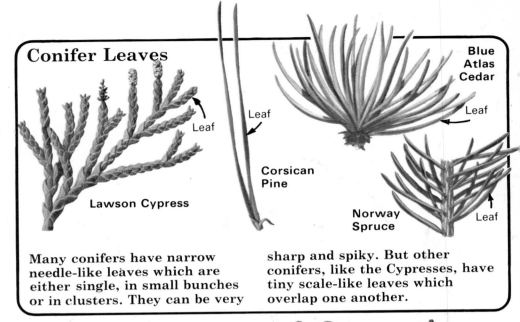

Many conifers have narrow needle-like leaves which are either single, in small bunches or in clusters. They can be very sharp and spiky. But other conifers, like the Cypresses, have tiny scale-like leaves which overlap one another.

Broadleaves

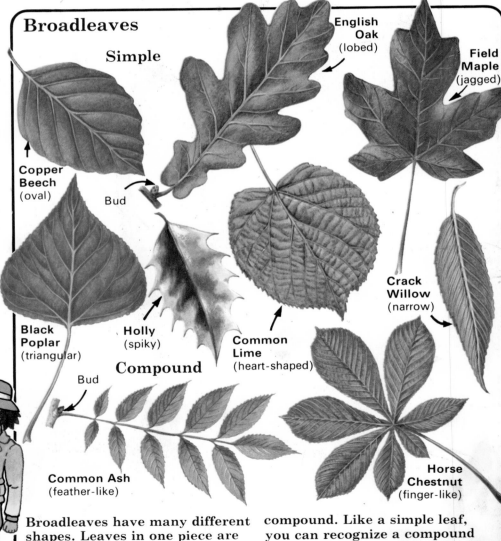

Broadleaves have many different shapes. Leaves in one piece are called simple, while those made up of many leaflets are called compound. Like a simple leaf, you can recognize a compound leaf because it only has one bud at the base of its stem.

These leaves are not drawn to the same scale.

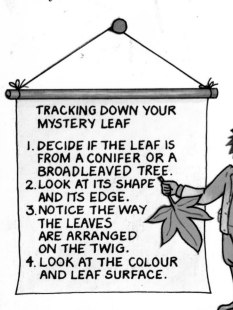

TRACKING DOWN YOUR MYSTERY LEAF

1. DECIDE IF THE LEAF IS FROM A CONIFER OR A BROADLEAVED TREE.
2. LOOK AT ITS SHAPE AND ITS EDGE.
3. NOTICE THE WAY THE LEAVES ARE ARRANGED ON THE TWIG.
4. LOOK AT THE COLOUR AND LEAF SURFACE.

Twigs

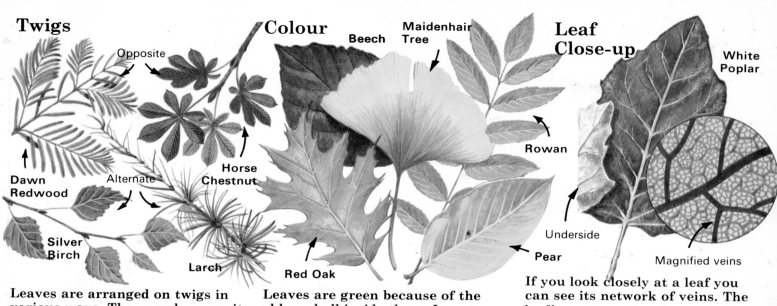

Dawn Redwood
Silver Birch
Opposite
Alternate
Horse Chestnut
Larch

Colour

Beech
Maidenhair Tree
Rowan
Pear
Red Oak

Leaf Close-up

White Poplar
Underside
Magnified veins

Leaves are arranged on twigs in various ways. They can be opposite each other in pairs, or they can be single and alternate from one side of the twig to the other.

Leaves are green because of the chlorophyll inside them. In autumn, the chlorophyll in broadleaves decays. They change colour before they fall.

If you look closely at a leaf you can see its network of veins. The leaf's upper surface is tough and often glossy to stop the sun from drying out the leaf. The underside is often hairy.

Leaf Scrapbook

Leaf skeleton

Keep a notebook of the leaves you find. Place each leaf between two sheets of paper. Then put them between books with a heavy object

on top. Leave them for a week. When the leaves are flat and dry, mount them in a notebook with tiny pieces of sellotape. Label the leaves and write down where and

when you found them. You may also find leaf skeletons, from which the dried leaf has crumbled away, leaving only the strong stem and veins.

Leaf Tiles

Press the leaf on to the "clay" with a rolling pin.

The finished tile can be painted or varnished.

Make your clay by mixing together:
2 cups flour (not self-raising)
1 cup salt
1 cup water

2 tablespoons cooking oil
Shape your "clay" into a ball. Roll it out with a rolling pin until it is about 2 cm thick. Press your leaf, vein side down, on to the clay so

that it leaves a mark. Remove the leaf and bake in the oven at Gas Mark ½ (250°F) for about two hours.

Winter Buds

Most broadleaved trees have no leaves in winter, but you can still identify them by their winter buds.

A winter bud contains the beginnings of next year's shoot, leaves and flowers. The thick, overlapping bud scales protect the shoot from the cold and from attack by insects. In places where winter is the dry season, the bud scales keep the new shoot from drying out. If the undeveloped leaf does not have bud scales, it may be covered with furry hairs to protect it.

In spring, when it gets warmer, the new shoot swells and breaks open the hard protective scales. Each year's shoot comes from a bud and ends by forming a new bud at the end of the growing season.

There are many buds on a twig. The leading bud, which is usually at the tip, contains the shoot which will grow most. The shoot becomes a twig and eventually a branch. The other buds hold leaves and flowers. They are also reserves in case the leading bud is damaged.

Inside a bud there are tiny leaves and flowers, all folded up. If you cut a bud in half and look at it through a lens, you can see the different parts.

This is a three-year-old Horse Chestnut twig. You can tell its age by counting the girdle scars. It has large brown buds in opposite pairs. The bud scales are sticky.

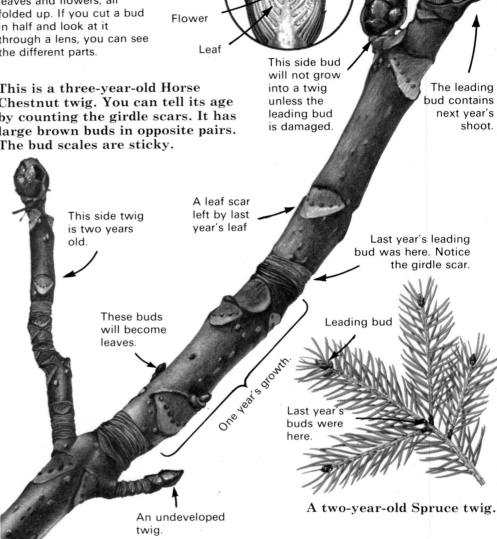

Outer scales of bud

Flower

Leaf

This side bud will not grow into a twig unless the leading bud is damaged.

The leading bud contains next year's shoot.

This side twig is two years old.

A leaf scar left by last year's leaf

Last year's leading bud was here. Notice the girdle scar.

These buds will become leaves.

One year's growth.

An undeveloped twig.

Leading bud

Last year's buds were here.

A two-year-old Spruce twig.

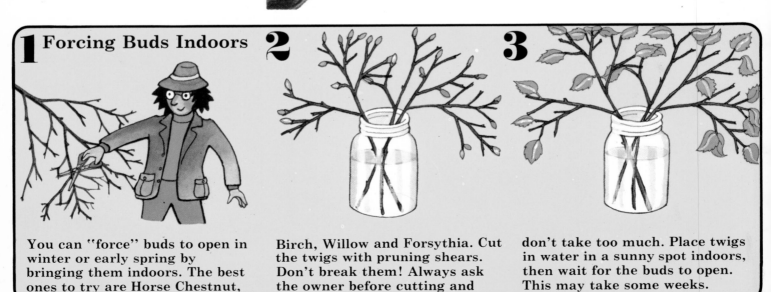

1 Forcing Buds Indoors

2

3

You can "force" buds to open in winter or early spring by bringing them indoors. The best ones to try are Horse Chestnut,

Birch, Willow and Forsythia. Cut the twigs with pruning shears. Don't break them! Always ask the owner before cutting and

don't take too much. Place twigs in water in a sunny spot indoors, then wait for the buds to open. This may take some weeks.

Winter Bud Identification Chart

What to Look for

If you try to identify trees by their winter buds, you will see that they vary a great deal. Here is a list of things to look for:

1 How are the buds positioned on the twig? Like leaves, buds can be in opposite pairs or single and alternate.
2 What colour are the buds and the twig?
3 What shape is the twig? Are the buds pointed or rounded?
4 Is the bud covered with hairs or scales? If there are scales, how many? Is the bud sticky?

Ash—Smooth, grey twig. Large, black buds opposite.

Sycamore— Large, green, opposite buds with dark-edged scales.

Beech—Slender twig. Alternate, spiky, brown buds sticking out.

Willow—Slender twig. Alternate buds close to twig.

False Acacia—Grey twig. Thorns next to tiny, alternate buds.

Elm—Zigzag twig. Alternate, blackish-red buds.

Lime—Zigzag twig. Alternate, reddish buds with two scales.

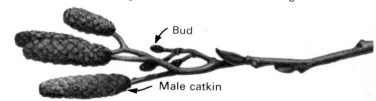

Bud

Male catkin

Alder—Alternate, stalked, purple buds often with male catkins.

Walnut—Thick, hollow twig. Big, black, velvety, alternate buds.

White Poplar—Twig and alternate buds covered with white down.

Turkey Oak—Clusters of alternate, whiskered buds.

Sweet Chestnut—Knobbly twig. Large, reddish, alternate buds.

Wild Cherry—Large, glossy, red buds grouped at tip of twig.

Plane—Alternate, cone-shaped buds. Ring scar around bud.

Magnolia—Huge, furry, green-grey buds.

Whitebeam—Downy, green, alternate buds.

These twigs are drawn life size.

Shape

Look at all these different tree shapes. Each type of tree has its own typical shape which depends on the arrangement of its branches. Winter is the best time of year to see the shapes of broadleaved trees because their branches are not hidden by leaves.

Practise making quick shape sketches when you are outside.

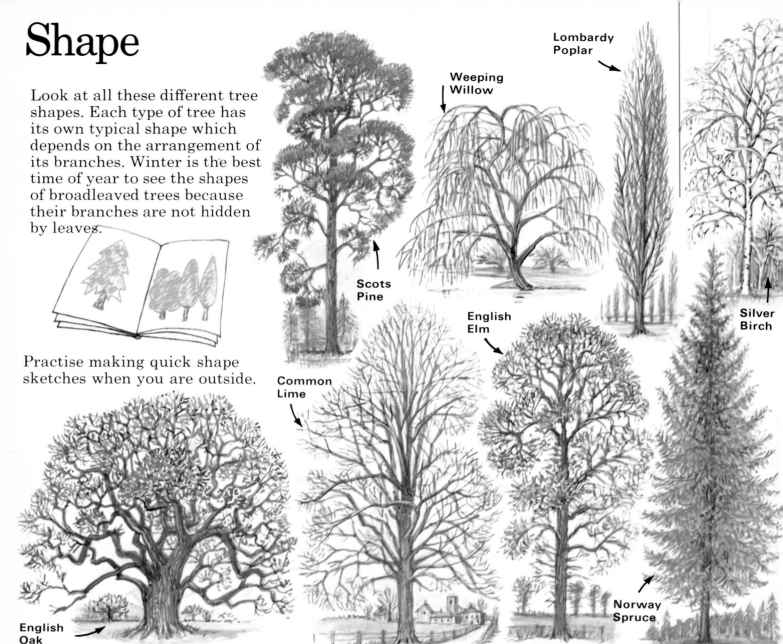

Weeping Willow

Lombardy Poplar

Scots Pine

English Elm

Silver Birch

Common Lime

English Oak

Norway Spruce

How Trees are Shaped

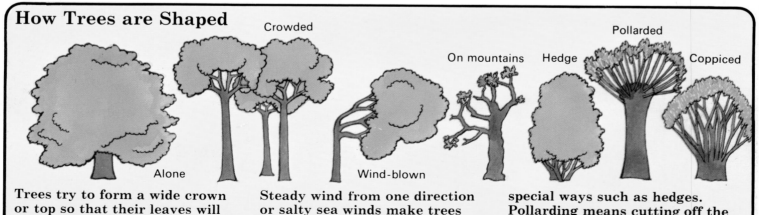

Crowded

Alone

Wind-blown

On mountains

Hedge

Pollarded

Coppiced

Trees try to form a wide crown or top so that their leaves will get lots of sunlight. Where trees are close together, they grow narrow to reach the light. Weather changes tree shapes.

Steady wind from one direction or salty sea winds make trees grow one-sided. On mountains, trees are dwarfed and gnarled by the cold and drying wind. Trees are also pruned or cut to grow in

special ways such as hedges. Pollarding means cutting off the branches of a tree. Coppicing is cutting the trunk down to the ground. This causes long, new shoots to grow.

Bark

The outside of the tree trunk is covered in a hard, tough layer of bark. It protects the inside of the tree from drying out and from damage by insects or animals. It also insulates the tree from extremes of heat and cold. Under the bark there are tubes carrying food (sap) which can be damaged if the bark is stripped off. If this happens, the tree may die.

When the tree is young the bark is thin and smooth, but with age it thickens and forms different patterns. You can identify trees by their bark.

Birch bark peels off in ribbon-like strips.

English Oak bark has deep ridges and cracks.

How Bark Patterns Form

The old bark splits and new bark forms underneath.

Bark is dead and cannot grow or stretch. As wood inside the bark grows outwards, the bark splits, peels or cracks in a way that is special to each type of tree.

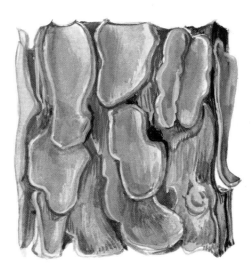

Scots Pine bark flakes off in large pieces.

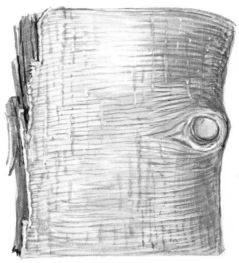

Beech has smooth thin bark, which flakes off in tiny pieces.

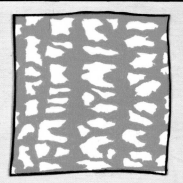

To make bark rubbings you need strong thin paper, sellotape and wax crayons or heel-ball. Tape the paper to the tree. Rub firmly with the crayon but do not tear the paper. Watch the bark pattern appear.

You can also rub the paper with candle wax. At home, paint over the rubbing. The bark pattern will stay white.

Cork

The bark on the Cork Oak is so thick that it can be removed without damaging the tree. Cork is used in many ways to keep in moisture and to resist heat.

Flowers

All trees produce flowers in order to make seeds that can grow into new trees. The flowers vary from tree to tree in size, shape and colour. Some are so small that you may not have noticed them.

Flowers have male parts called stamens and female parts called ovaries. The stamen produces pollen, while the ovary contains ovules. When pollen from the stamen reaches the ovules in the ovary, the flower is fertilized. Fertilized flowers grow into fruits (see pages 16–17), which contain seeds.

Flowers with both ovaries and stamens in the same flower, like the Cherry, are called perfect. On other trees the ovaries and the stamens are in separate flowers. Clusters of all-female flowers grow together and so do all-male flowers. The clusters can be cone-shaped or long and dangling (these are called catkins). A few trees, such as Yew, Holly and Willow, have their male and female flowers on entirely separate trees.

Parts of a Flower

Petal

The top of the ovary is called the stigma.

Ovary with ovules

Stamen with pollen

Stalk

Sepal

This is a cross-section of a Cherry blossom, which is a typical perfect flower. It has male and female parts.

European Larch

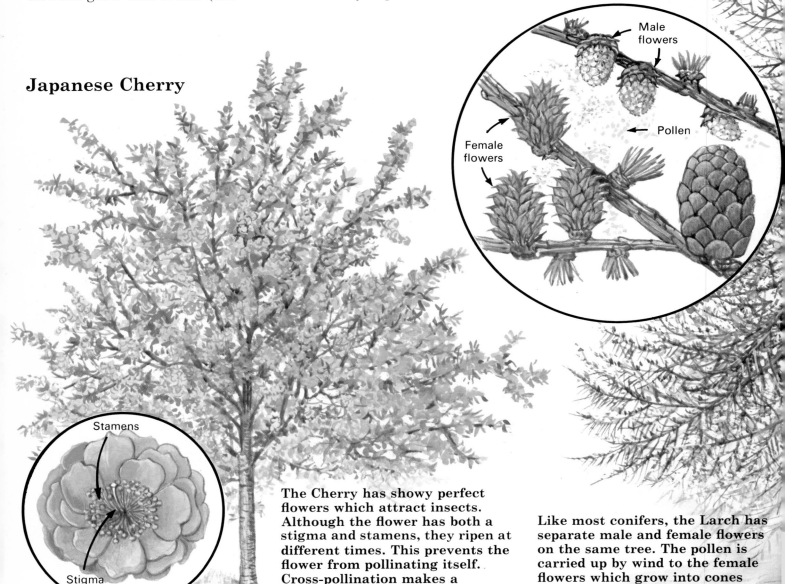

Male flowers

Female flowers

Pollen

Japanese Cherry

Stamens

Stigma

The Cherry has showy perfect flowers which attract insects. Although the flower has both a stigma and stamens, they ripen at different times. This prevents the flower from pollinating itself. Cross-pollination makes a healthier seed.

Like most conifers, the Larch has separate male and female flowers on the same tree. The pollen is carried up by wind to the female flowers which grow into cones when they are fertilized.

Pollination

Crab Apple

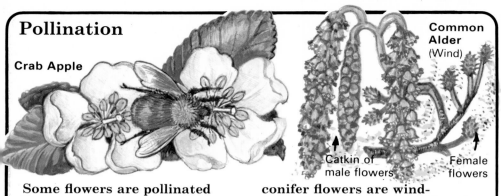

Common Alder (Wind)

Catkin of male flowers

Female flowers

Some flowers are pollinated by insects. Insects, feeding on flowers, accidentally pick up pollen on their bodies, and it rubs off on the next flower they visit. This is called cross-pollination. Most catkins and conifer flowers are wind-pollinated. They are small and dull because they do not need to attract insects. The wind blows pollen off the long stamens and the sticky stigmas catch the pollen.

Fertilization

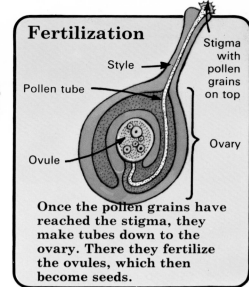

Style

Stigma with pollen grains on top

Pollen tube

Ovary

Ovule

Once the pollen grains have reached the stigma, they make tubes down to the ovary. There they fertilize the ovules, which then become seeds.

Crack Willow

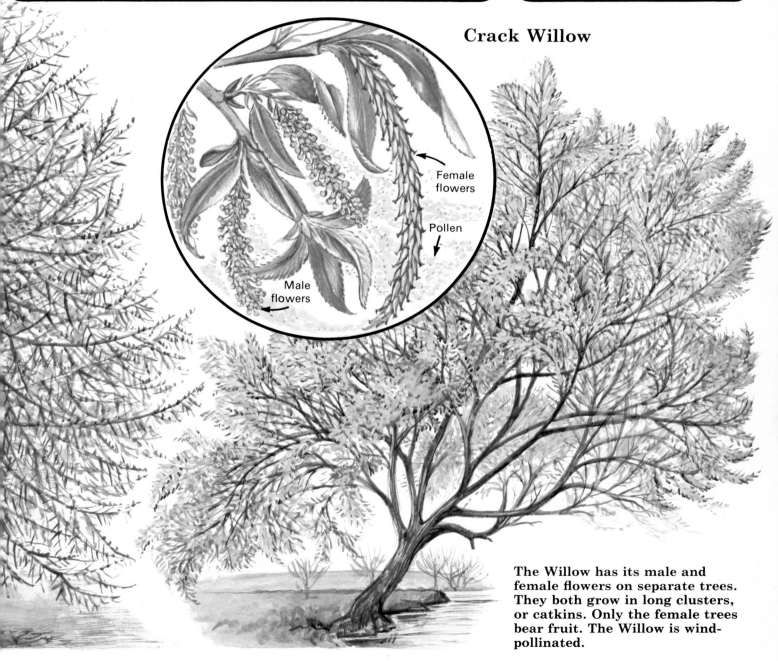

Female flowers

Pollen

Male flowers

The Willow has its male and female flowers on separate trees. They both grow in long clusters, or catkins. Only the female trees bear fruit. The Willow is wind-pollinated.

Fruits and Seeds

Fruits containing seeds grow from fertilized flowers. An Apple and the prickly conker case of the Horse Chestnut are both fruits. Although they look different, they do the same job. They protect the seeds they carry and help them to spread to a place where they can grow.

Conifers bear fruits whose seeds are uncovered, but which are usually held in a scaly cone. Broadleaved trees have fruits which completely surround their seeds. They take the form of nuts, berries, soft fruits, and many other kinds.

Many fruits and cones are damaged by insects and disease, are eaten by birds and animals, or fall off the trees before they can ripen. The seeds inside the remaining fruits ripen in the autumn. They need to get far away from the parent tree, or it will take all the food and light.

Seeds are spread by birds, animals, wind and water. Very few seeds ever get to a place where they can reach full growth. About one in a million acorns becomes an Oak tree.

How a Cone Ripens

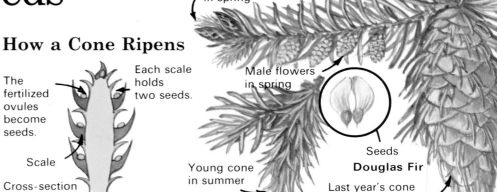

The fertilized ovules become seeds.

Scale

Each scale holds two seeds.

Cross-section of a cone.

Female flowers in spring

Male flowers in spring

Young cone in summer

Seeds

Douglas Fir

Last year's cone which is now empty

Cones develop from the female flowers. After pollination, the scales harden and close. The stalk often bends, so the cone hangs down. The cone turns from green to brown. When the seeds are ripe and the weather is warm and dry, the scales open. The seeds flutter out on papery wings. Most cones stay on the tree for a year. Others take two years to ripen, and some remain long after the seeds have been dropped.

Scots Pine

Cones open in warm, dry weather to release their seeds. If it is wet, the scales close. Find a cone and make it open by placing it near a heater. Then put it in a damp place, and it will close.

Fruits of Conifers

Most cones have woody scales and vary in size from 1 cm to 35 cm and can weigh as much as 2 kg. See how many different kinds of cones you can collect.

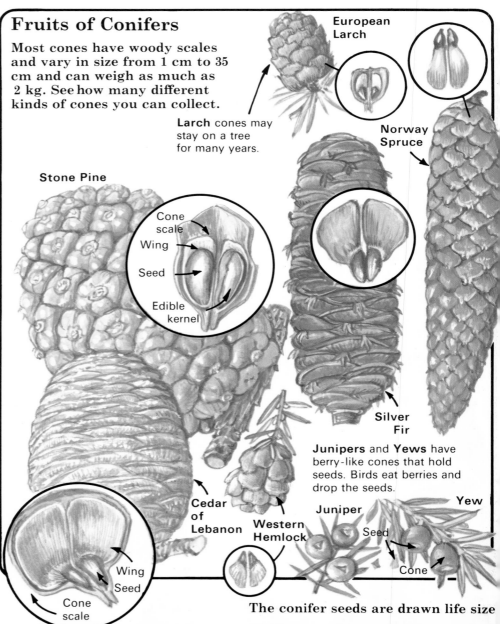

European Larch

Larch cones may stay on a tree for many years.

Norway Spruce

Stone Pine

Cone scale
Wing
Seed
Edible kernel

Silver Fir

Junipers and Yews have berry-like cones that hold seeds. Birds eat berries and drop the seeds.

Cedar of Lebanon

Western Hemlock

Juniper

Yew

Seed

Cone

Wing
Seed
Cone scale

The conifer seeds are drawn life size

How a Peach Ripens

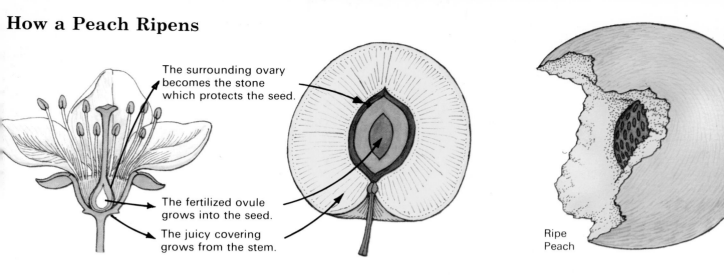

The surrounding ovary becomes the stone which protects the seed.

The fertilized ovule grows into the seed.

The juicy covering grows from the stem.

Ripe Peach

The pictures above show how the different parts of a flower grow into the different parts of a fruit. The flower is a Peach blossom.

Water from the stem and sunshine make the fleshy part of the fruit swell. As the fruit ripens, it turns golden pink and softens. The

bright colour and sweet smell attract hungry animals or people who eat the juicy outer layer and throw away the stone.

Fruits of Broadleaved Trees

Broadleaved trees produce many different kinds of fruits. Some are nuts with hard outer shells, some are soft fruits, some are pods, and some have wings or hairs.

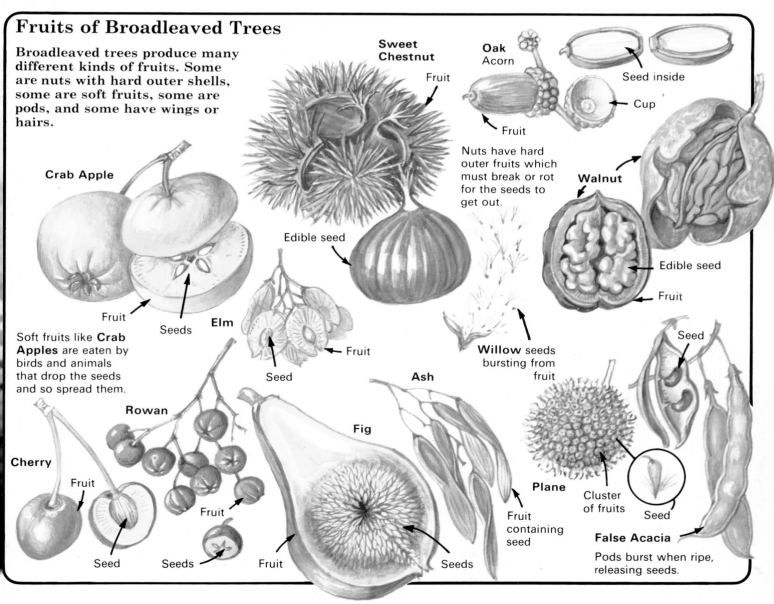

Sweet Chestnut
Fruit

Oak Acorn
Seed inside
Cup
Fruit

Nuts have hard outer fruits which must break or rot for the seeds to get out.

Walnut
Edible seed
Fruit

Crab Apple
Fruit
Seeds

Edible seed

Soft fruits like **Crab Apples** are eaten by birds and animals that drop the seeds and so spread them.

Elm
Fruit
Seed

Willow seeds bursting from fruit

Seed

Rowan
Fruit

Ash

Cherry
Fruit
Seed

Fig

Fruit
Seeds

Plane
Cluster of fruits
Seed

Fruit containing seed

Seeds
Seeds
Fruit
Seeds

False Acacia
Pods burst when ripe, releasing seeds.

The cones and fruits are drawn two thirds life size.

Grow Your Own Seedling

Try growing your own tree from a seed. Pick ripe seeds from trees or collect them from the ground if you know that they are fresh. The time a seed takes to sprout varies, but an acorn takes about two months. Some seeds, like those from conifers, may need to lie in the ground for over a year. Once your seedling has sprouted, keep a diary of its growth with drawings or photographs.

What You Need

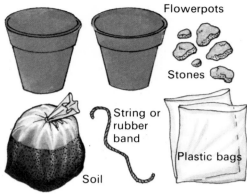

Flowerpots

Stones

String or rubber band

Plastic bags

Soil

What to Plant

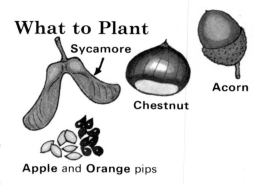

Sycamore

Chestnut

Acorn

Apple and Orange pips

Here are some seeds which are easy to grow. Acorns are usually successful, but try anything!

1

Soak acorns or other hard nuts in warm water overnight. Peel off the hard outer shells if you can, but do not try to cut the shells off acorns.

2

Put a handful of stones in the bottom of your pot. This is to help the water to drain properly. Place a saucer under the pot.

3

Put some soil, or compost, on top of the stones until the pot is about two thirds full. Water the soil until it is moist but not soggy.

4

Place the acorns or other seeds on top of the soil. They need lots of room to grow, so only put one acorn in each pot.

5

Cover the acorns or other seeds with a layer of soil about as thick as the seeds.

6

Fasten with string or rubber band.

Place a plastic bag over the pot and fasten it. This will keep the seed moist without watering. Put the pot in a sunny place and wait.

7

As soon as you see the seedling appear, remove the plastic bag. Water the seedling once or twice a week. The soil should be moist, but not wet.

8

Put your seedling outside in the summer if you can. In autumn, it will be ready to be planted in the ground (or you can leave it in its pot).

9

Dig a hole a bit larger than the pot. Gently scoop out the seedling and the soil around it from the pot. Plant it in the hole, pat down the soil on top, and water it.

Forestry

Trees have been growing on Earth for about 350 million years. The land was once covered by natural forests, but they have been cut down for timber and cleared for land. New forests are planted to replace the trees that are cut down.

Because conifers grow faster than broadleaved trees and produce straight timber, they are preferred for wood production.

Seedbeds

The seeds are sown in seedbeds. When the seedlings are 15-20cm high, they are planted in rows in another bed where they have more room. They are weeded regularly.

Planting Out

When the seedlings are about 50cm high, they are planted out in the forest ground, which has been cleared and ploughed. There are about 2,500 trees per hectare.

This picture and the two above show the story of a Douglas Fir plantation, and what the foresters do to care for the trees.

Fire towers on hills help to spot fire—the forest's worst enemy. Fires can be started by a carelessly dropped match or an unguarded campfire.

Trees can be sprayed with herbicides or treated with fertilizers from the air.

When the trees are felled, they are taken away to sawmills to be cut up.

Every few years the poorer trees are cut out to give more light and room to the stronger ones. These thinnings are used for poles or are made into paper pulp.

Dead and lower branches are cut off trees. This lessens the risk of fire and stops knots from forming in the wood.

Trees are felled when they are full-grown (about 70 years for conifers and 150 years for Oaks). About one in every ten trees reaches its full growth.

Annual Rings

Inside the bark is the wood which is made up of many layers (see page 7). Each year the cambium makes a ring of wood on its inner side and grows outwards. This layer is called an annual ring. The early wood made in spring is pale and has wide tubes to carry sap. Late wood, which is formed in summer, is darker and stronger. In wet years, the layers of wood are broad and the annual rings are far apart, but in dry years they are narrow. They are also narrow if the trees are not thinned.

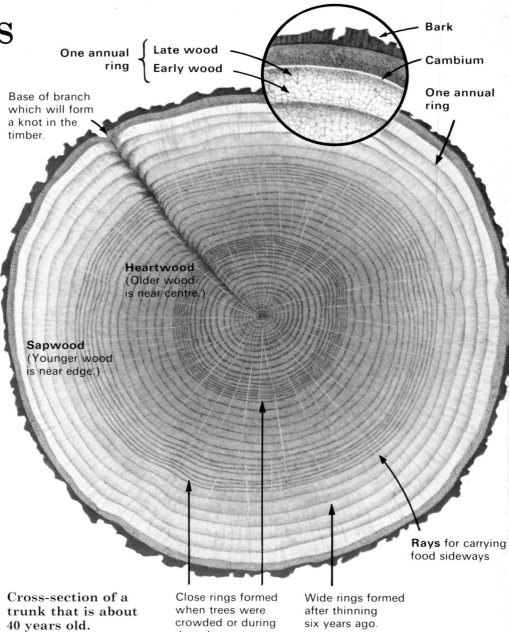

One annual ring { Late wood / Early wood

Bark

Cambium

One annual ring

Base of branch which will form a knot in the timber.

Heartwood (Older wood is near centre.)

Sapwood (Younger wood is near edge.)

Rays for carrying food sideways

Cross-section of a trunk that is about 40 years old.

Close rings formed when trees were crowded or during drought.

Wide rings formed after thinning six years ago.

Palms

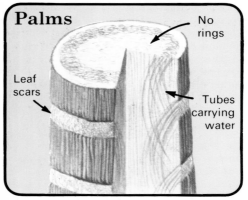

No rings

Leaf scars

Tubes carrying water

Palm trees do not have annual rings because they have no cambium to grow new wood. Their trunks are like giant stalks which do not grow thicker.

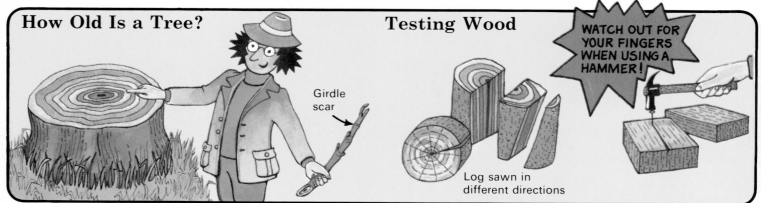

How Old Is a Tree?

Girdle scar

Testing Wood

WATCH OUT FOR YOUR FINGERS WHEN USING A HAMMER!

Log sawn in different directions

You can find out the age of a tree by counting the annual rings in a cross-section of its trunk. It is easiest to count the dark rings of late wood. Twigs also have annual layers. Cut off a twig on the slant and count its rings. Then count the girdle scars on the outside. Do they agree?

Saw a small log in different ways and look at the patterns the wood makes. Test the strength of different woods by hammering nails into them.

Wood

The wood inside different types of trees varies in colour and pattern just as their outside appearances vary. Different kinds of wood are especially suited for certain uses. Wood from conifers, called softwood, is mainly used for building and paper pulp, while broadleaved trees, called hardwoods, are used to make furniture.

At the sawmill, the person operating the saw decides the best way to cut each log. A log can be made into many different sizes of planks as well as into paper pulp.

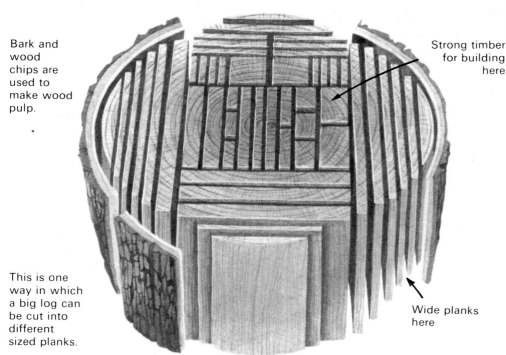

Bark and wood chips are used to make wood pulp.

Strong timber for building here

This is one way in which a big log can be cut into different sized planks.

Wide planks here

Grain

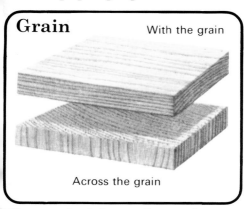

With the grain

Across the grain

When a plank is cut from a log, the annual rings make vertical lines which may be wavy or straight. This pattern is called the grain. Wood cut with the grain is stronger.

Knots

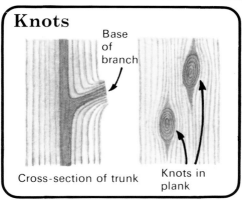

Base of branch

Cross-section of trunk

Knots in plank

In a plank you may see dark spots called knots. These were where the base of a branch was buried in the trunk of the tree. This distorts the grain, leaving a knot.

Seasoning

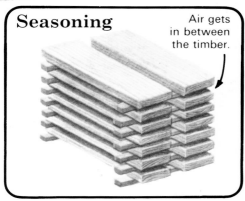

Air gets in between the timber.

Fresh wood contains water which is why green logs spit in the fire. As wood dries, it shrinks and often cracks or warps. Planks must be dried out, or seasoned, before they can be used.

Processed Wood

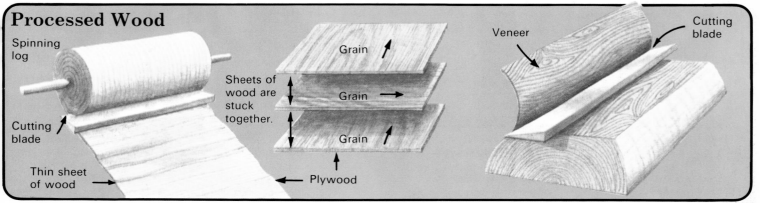

Spinning log

Cutting blade

Thin sheet of wood

Grain

Grain

Grain

Sheets of wood are stuck together.

Plywood

Veneer

Cutting blade

Much of the wood that you see around you has been 'processed'. Plywood is thin layers of wood which are glued together with the grain lying in different directions.

It is stronger than ordinary wood and does not warp. The thin sheet of wood is peeled off the log like a Swiss roll. Veneer is a thin sheet of wood with a beautiful grain

which is used on the surface of plain furniture. Chipboard (not shown) is made of small chips and shavings mixed with glue.

Pests and Fungi

Trees are attacked by insects and fungus diseases. Insects use trees for food, shelter and as places to breed. They can cause serious damage to trees, but they rarely kill them.

Fungi are a group of non-flowering plants which include mushrooms. Because fungi cannot make their own food, they may feed off other living things and sometimes kill them. Fungi spread by releasing microscopic seeds, called spores, into the air. If these spores get into the tree and spread, they will rot it.

Leaves and Shoots

Spangle Galls

Cherry Galls

Pine Looper

Gall Wasp

Green Tortrix

Pine Sawfly

Kidney Galls

The **Tent Caterpillar** lives in a "tent" which it spins among the branches.

Oak Apple Galls

Larva

Nut Weevils lay their eggs inside nuts, where the larvae grow.

Adult **Nut Weevil**

Many moth and butterfly caterpillars and other larvae eat leaves. Often each species only feeds on a certain type of tree.

Leaf Miner

Leaf Roller

Aphid

Leaf Miners eat tunnels through leaves. **Leaf Rollers** fold leaves over themselves for protection.

Some insects lay their eggs in leaves or shoots. The tree forms swellings, called galls, around the eggs. The larvae feed inside the galls.

"Pineapple" Gall

An **Aphid** made this "pineapple" gall by piercing a shoot to suck out the sap.

Bark and Wood

Conifer Heart Rot is caused by this bracket fungus. It attacks conifers and rots the inside of trees until they die.

White Pine Blister Rust is a fungus which causes swellings on pine trunks or branches.

Look for **Scale** insects on bark. If you pull one off, you may see the grub which sucks sap from the tree.

Elm Bark Beetles make tunnels under Elm bark. They spread the fungus which causes Dutch Elm Disease.

Honey Fungus attacks the roots of many trees. In autumn, the toadstools appear at the base of infected ones.

The **Pine Weevil** strips the bark off newly planted conifers.

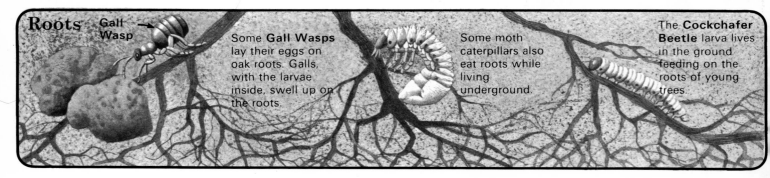

Roots

Gall Wasp

Some **Gall Wasps** lay their eggs on oak roots. Galls, with the larvae inside, swell up on the roots.

Some moth caterpillars also eat roots while living underground.

The **Cockchafer Beetle** larva lives in the ground feeding on the roots of young trees.

Keeping an Oak Gall

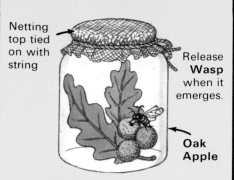

Netting top tied on with string

Release **Wasp** when it emerges.

Oak Apple

In summer, collect Oak Apples and other galls which do not have holes in them. Keep them in a jar with netting on top. The wasps living inside the galls should emerge in a month.

Making Spore Prints

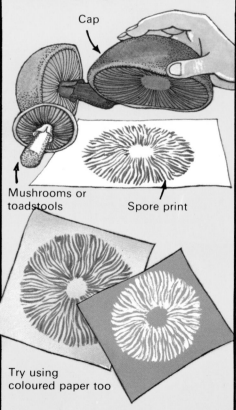

Cap

Mushrooms or toadstools

Spore print

Try using coloured paper too

Make spore prints from mushrooms. Cut off the stalk and place the cap on some paper. Leave it overnight. It will release its spores on the paper, leaving a print. Always wash your hands after handling fungus.

Injuries

Bark stripped by a **Deer's** antlers

Tree struck by lightning

Bark gnawed by a **Field Vole**

Sometimes trees are damaged by animals. Deer strip the bark off trees when they scrape the "velvet" off their antlers. Squirrels, voles and rabbits eat young bark. If lightning strikes a tree, the trunk often cracks. This happens because the sap gets so hot that it becomes steam. It expands and then explodes, shattering the tree.

How a Tree Heals Itself

Recent pruning cut

Three years later

Six years later

Bare wood

New bark covering wound

If a branch is pruned off a tree properly, the wound usually heals. A new rim of bark grows from the cambium around the cut. This finished seal will keep out fungus and disease. It takes years for a wound to heal. But if a wound completely surrounds the trunk, the tree will die because its food supply is cut off.

How Trees Die

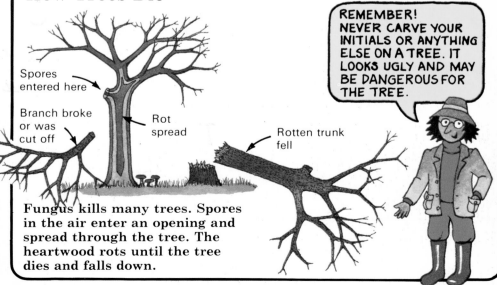

Spores entered here

Branch broke or was cut off

Rot spread

Rotten trunk fell

REMEMBER! NEVER CARVE YOUR INITIALS OR ANYTHING ELSE ON A TREE. IT LOOKS UGLY AND MAY BE DANGEROUS FOR THE TREE.

Fungus kills many trees. Spores in the air enter an opening and spread through the tree. The heartwood rots until the tree dies and falls down.

Woodland Life

When you walk in a forest, it may seem dead and deserted, but in its depths, the forest hides a wealth of life. Trees provide protection from bad weather, wind and too much sun. Tree roots help to hold the soil in place. Fallen leaves and twigs make a rich soil called humus. All this encourages plants to grow.

Trees also provide food and shelter for many animals. The plants and animals you find in coniferous and broadleaved forests are usually different, although they may overlap.

A Coniferous Forest

A coniferous forest is dark and dense. Few plants grow on the ground because of the thick layer of needles and the lack of light. Here are some animals and plants you might see in a coniferous forest.

Pine Marten

Squirrel's drey

Long-eared Owl's nest

Long-eared Owl

Great Spotted Woodpecker

Red Deer

Crossbill

Bracken

Fox

Black Grouse

Norway Spruce cones

Wood Ant-hill

Broad Buckler Fern

Timberman

Goldcrest

Red Squirrel

Fly Agaric

Lichen

Black Slug

Treecreeper

A Broadleaved Forest

A broadleaved forest is more light and open and so attracts many plants and animals. There are many flowers in spring before the trees' leaves have blocked out the light. As you can see, an Oak wood supports a great variety of life.

Mistletoe

Green Woodpecker

Nuthatch

Rook in nest

Tawny Owl

Long-eared Bat in tree

Poor Man's Beefsteak

Blue Tit

Oak

Wood Anemone

Roe Deer

Badger

Bluebells

Rabbit

Pheasant

Hedgehog

Common Shrew

Ivy

Primrose

Common Toad

Earthworm

Greater Stag Beetle

Speckled Wood Butterfly

Making a Tree Survey

Make a survey of the trees that grow around you. Choose a garden, street or park where you think there will be a variety of trees, but start with a small area first. It is easier and more fun to do this with a friend.

When you have decided on an area, make a rough map of it with any landmarks, such as roads or buildings. Try to work out a scale for your map. (It helps to use graph paper.) Work in a definite order so that you do not miss out any trees, and then go back to identify and measure them.

What to Take

Tape measure

Pencils

Tree field guide

String

Notebook

Identifying a Tree

Try to identify the trees using this book or a field guide. Remember that there are many clues to help you recognize them, so don't use just one clue.

Making a Map

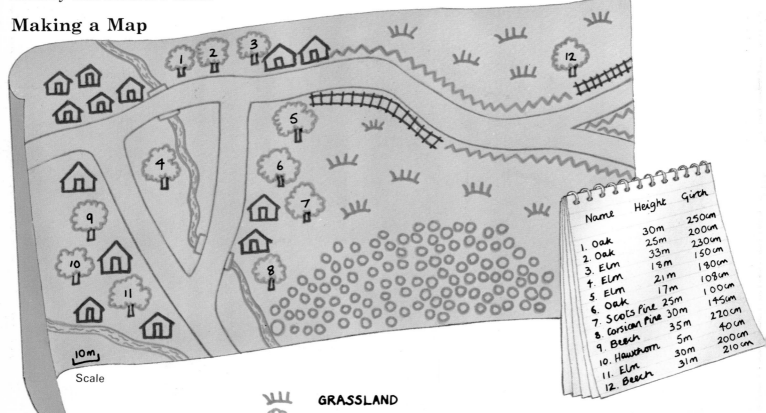

Scale 10m

Name	Height	Girth
1. Oak	30m	250cm
2. Oak	25m	200cm
3. Elm	33m	230cm
4. Elm	18m	150cm
5. Elm	21m	180cm
6. Oak	17m	108cm
7. Scots Pine	25m	100cm
8. Corsican Pine	30m	145cm
9. Beech	35m	220cm
10. Hawthorn	5m	40cm
11. Elm	30m	200cm
12. Beech	31m	210cm

GRASSLAND

TREE

WOODLAND

STREAM

BRIDGE

HOUSE

HEDGE

FENCE

After you have identified and measured the trees (as shown above), make a neater and more detailed copy of your map. Show the scale of your map. Then make a key to the symbols you used. Here are some suggestions:

Then write down the findings of your survey. Give the name, height and girth of each tree. Repeat the survey later to see if there are any new trees, or if anything has changed. If you enjoy making the survey, you can write to The Council for Protection of Rural England to find out how to do a more complicated one.

Measuring a Tree

Mark stick here

Your friend is 1.5 m tall.

The tree is four times the height of your friend. It is 6 m tall.

Ask your friend to stand next to the tree. Hold a stick up vertically at arm's length, and move your thumb up the stick until it is in line with your friend's feet, while the tip of the stick is in line with the top of your friend's head.

Mark the stick where your thumb is. See how many times the part of the stick above the mark goes into the height of the tree (four times here). Then multiply your friend's height (1.5 m here) by this number to get the height of the tree (6 m).

Measure around the tree at chest height to find the girth. Ask your friend to hold one end of some string while you hold the other. Walk around the tree until you meet. Then measure the length of string.

1 Studying a Tree

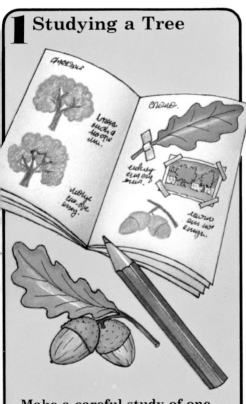

Make a careful study of one tree all through the year. Choose a tree which you can get to easily and often. Make a notebook in which you keep a record of when it comes into leaf, when it flowers and fruits, and when it drops its leaves. Include sketches or photos of the tree at these different times and specimens from it.

2

Study the animals that live in or near your tree. Look for birds' nests and squirrels' dreys in the tree top. Look on the trunk for insects and on the ground for other traces of animals, such as owl pellets, and nuts or cones which have been eaten by animals. To examine the insects in the tree top, beat a sturdy branch with a stick. Catch the insects that fall on a white sheet.

3

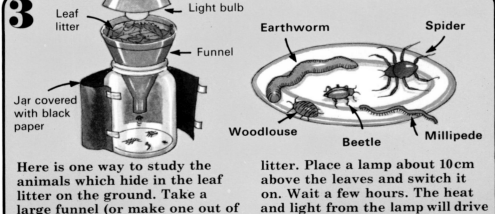

Leaf litter

Light bulb

Funnel

Jar covered with black paper

Earthworm

Spider

Woodlouse

Beetle

Millipede

Here is one way to study the animals which hide in the leaf litter on the ground. Take a large funnel (or make one out of tin foil), and place it in a jar. Cover the jar with black paper. Fill the funnel with damp leaf litter. Place a lamp about 10 cm above the leaves and switch it on. Wait a few hours. The heat and light from the lamp will drive the animals into the dark jar. You can take them out and study them.

Common Trees to Spot : Conifers

Lawson Cypress 25 m. Narrow shape. Drooping top shoot. Small, round cones. Common as hedge.

Western Red Cedar 30 m. Branches curve upwards. Tiny, flower-like cones. Hedges.

Yew 15 m. Dark green. Trunk gnarled. Bark reddish. Leaves and red-berried fruits poisonous.

Western Hemlock 35 m. Branches and top shoot droop. Small cones. Needles various lengths.

Norway Spruce 30 m. Christmas tree. Long, hanging cones. Parks, gardens, plantations.

Douglas Fir 40 m. Hanging, shaggy cones. Deep-ridged bark. Important timber tree.

European Silver Fir 40 m. Large, upright cones at top of tree. Parklands.

Scots Pine 35 m. Uneven crown. Bare trunk. Flaking bark. Common wild and planted.

Corsican Pine 36 m. Shape rounder and fuller than **Scots Pine.** Long, dark-green needles. Dark brown bark.

Blue Atlas Cedar 25 m. Broad shape. Barrel-shaped, upright cones. Blue-green needles. Parks.

European Larch 38 m. Upright cones egg-shaped. Soft, light-green needles fall off in winter.

Japanese Larch 35 m. Upright, rosette-like cones. Orange twigs. Blue-green needles fall off in winter.

Broadleaved Trees

Olive 10 m. Evergreen. Twisted grey trunk. Black edible fruits. Southern Europe.

Holm Oak 20 m. Evergreen. Shiny leaves resemble Holly. Grey bark. Parks and gardens.

Weeping Willow 20 m. Drooping shape. Near water and in gardens.

Japanese Cherry 9 m. Flowers April—May. Many varieties. Gardens and along streets.

Wild Cherry or **Gean** 15 m. Red-brown bark peels in ribbons. Flowers April—May. Fruits sour. Woods, thickets.

Almond 8 m. Flowers March—April before leaves. Edible nut inside green fruit. Gardens.

Holly 10 m. Evergreen. Leaves often variegated. Berries poisonous. Often shrub-like.

Sweet Chestnut 35 m. Spiral-ridged bark. Two edible nuts in prickly green case. Wide-spreading branches.

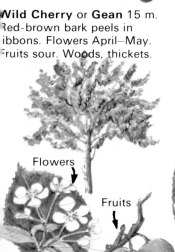

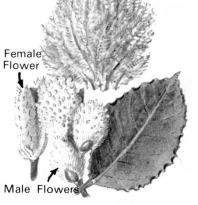

Crab Apple 10 m. Small tree. Flowers May. Fruits edible but sour. Wild in hedges and thickets.

Common Pear 15 m. Straight trunk. Flowers April—May. Edible fruits. Hedgerows and gardens.

Orange 9 m. Evergreen. Many varieties. Fragrant flowers in winter. Fruits edible. Southern Europe.

Goat or **Pussy Willow** 7 m. Catkins March—April. Separate male and female trees. Hedges and damp woodlands.

Broadleaved Trees

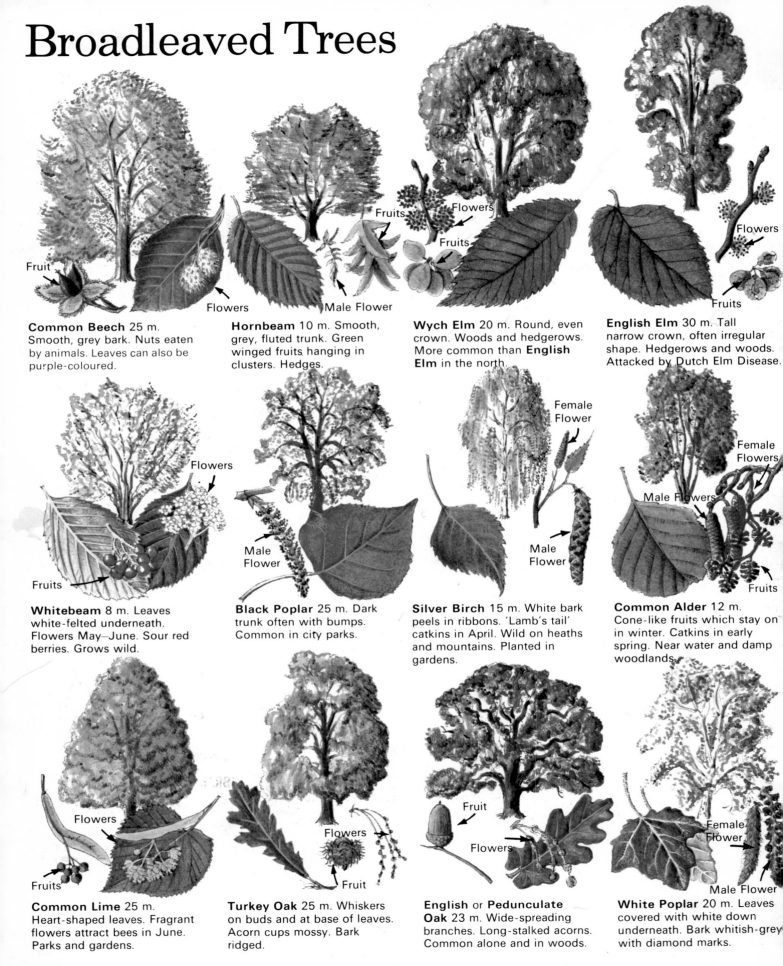

Common Beech 25 m. Smooth, grey bark. Nuts eaten by animals. Leaves can also be purple-coloured.

Fruit

Hornbeam 10 m. Smooth, grey, fluted trunk. Green winged fruits hanging in clusters. Hedges.

Flowers · Male Flower

Wych Elm 20 m. Round, even crown. Woods and hedgerows. More common than **English Elm** in the north.

Flowers · Fruits

English Elm 30 m. Tall narrow crown, often irregular shape. Hedgerows and woods. Attacked by Dutch Elm Disease.

Flowers · Fruits

Whitebeam 8 m. Leaves white-felted underneath. Flowers May–June. Sour red berries. Grows wild.

Flowers · Fruits

Black Poplar 25 m. Dark trunk often with bumps. Common in city parks.

Male Flower

Silver Birch 15 m. White bark peels in ribbons. 'Lamb's tail' catkins in April. Wild on heaths and mountains. Planted in gardens.

Female Flower · Male Flower

Common Alder 12 m. Cone-like fruits which stay on in winter. Catkins in early spring. Near water and damp woodlands.

Female Flowers · Male Flowers · Fruits

Common Lime 25 m. Heart-shaped leaves. Fragrant flowers attract bees in June. Parks and gardens.

Flowers · Fruits

Turkey Oak 25 m. Whiskers on buds and at base of leaves. Acorn cups mossy. Bark ridged.

Flowers · Fruit

English or **Pedunculate Oak** 23 m. Wide-spreading branches. Long-stalked acorns. Common alone and in woods.

Fruit · Flowers

White Poplar 20 m. Leaves covered with white down underneath. Bark whitish-grey with diamond marks.

Female Flower · Male Flower

Tulip Tree 20 m. Tulip-like flowers June-July. Upright brown fruits. Parks, gardens.

Field Maple 10 m. Rounded crown. Narrow-ridged bark. Winged seeds almost form straight line. Hedges and woods.

Norway Maple 15 m. Seeds form wide angle. Autumn leaves colourful. Parks, streets.

Sycamore 20 m. Seeds form close angle. Smooth bark flakes off in plates. Parks, streets.

London Plane 30 m. Bark flakes off leaving white patches. Spiky fruits stay on in winter. City streets.

Fig 6 m. Flower inside a pear-shaped receptacle which becomes the fruit. Gardens.

Horse Chestnut 25 m. Compound leaves. Upright flowers May. Prickly fruits with 'conkers' inside.

Laburnum or **Golden Rain** 7 m. Compound leaves. Flowers May-June. Seeds poisonous. Gardens.

False Acacia or **Locust Tree** 20 m. Compound leaves. Ridged twigs spiny. Hanging flowers in June. Gardens, parks.

Walnut 15 m. Compound leaves. Deep-ridged bark. Hollow twigs. Edible nuts inside thick green fruits.

Rowan or **Mountain Ash** 7 m. Compound leaves. Flowers May. Sour orange berries September. Wild on mountains.

Common Ash 25 m. Compound leaves open late. Keys stay on in winter. Common in woods and parks.

Index

Acacia, False, **11, 17, 31**
Alder, **11, 15, 30**
Almond, **29**
Ant, Wood, **24**
Aphid, **22**
Apple, **3, 18**
Ash, **8, 11, 17, 31**; Mountain, *see* Rowan

Badger, **25**
Bat, Long-eared, **25**
Beech, **4, 5, 9, 11, 13, 30**; Copper, **8**
Beetle, **27**; Cockchafer, **22**; Elm Bark, **22**; Greater Stag, **25**
Birch, Silver, **3, 9, 12, 13, 30**
Bluebell, **25**
Bracken, **24**
Butterfly, Speckled Wood, **25**

Cedar, Blue Atlas, **8, 28**; of Lebanon, **16**; Western Red, **28**
Cherry, **17**; Japanese, **14, 29**; Wild, **11, 29**
Chestnut, Horse, **5, 8, 9, 10, 31**; Red Horse, **2**; Sweet, **11, 17, 18, 29**
Conifer Heart Rot, **22**
Crab Apple, **15, 17, 29**
Crossbill, **24**
Cypress, Lawson, **8, 28**

Deer, Red, **24**; Roe, **25**

Earthworm, **25, 27**
Elm, English, **11, 12, 17, 30**; Wych, **30**

Fern, Broad Buckler, **24**
Fig, **17, 31**
Fir, Douglas, **16, 19, 28**; Silver, **16, 28**

Fly Agaric, **24**
Fox, **24**
Fungus, Bracket, **25**; Honey, **22**

Gall, Oak, **22, 23**; Wasp, **22, 23**
Gean, *see* Cherry, Wild
Goldcrest, **24**
Golden Rain, *see* Laburnum
Grouse, Black, **24**

Hazel, **5**
Hedgehog, **25**
Hemlock, Western, **16, 28**
Holly, **7, 8, 29**
Hornbeam, **30**

Ivy, **25**

Juniper, **16**

Laburnum, **31**
Larch, European, **5, 9, 14, 15, 16, 28**; Japanese, **28**
Leaf Miner, **22**
Leaf Roller, **22**
Lichen, **24**
Lime, **4, 8, 11, 12, 30**
Locust Tree, *see* Acacia, False

Magnolia, **11**
Maidenhair Tree, **9**
Maple, Field, **8, 31**; Japanese, **4, 29**; Norway, **2, 31**
Millipede, **27**
Mistletoe, **25**
Moss, **25**

Nuthatch, **25**

Oak, Cork, **13**; English or Pedunculate, **4, 5, 8, 12, 13, 17, 18, 22, 23, 25, 30**; Holm, **29**; Red, **9**; Turkey, **11, 30**
Olive, **29**
Orange, **18, 29**
Owl, Long-eared, **24**; Tawny, **25**
Palm, **5, 20**; Canary, **5**
Peach, **17**
Pear, **9, 29**
Pheasant, **25**
Pine, Corsican, **8, 28**; Scots, **5, 7, 12, 13, 16, 28**; Stone, **16**
Pine Looper, **22**
Pine Marten, **24**
Pine Sawfly, **22**
Plane, London, **11, 17, 31**
Poor Man's Beefsteak, **25**
Poplar, Black, **8, 30**; Lombardy, **4, 12**; White, **9, 11, 30**
Primrose, **25**

Rabbit, **25**
Redwood, Dawn, **9**
Rook, **25**
Rowan, **9, 17, 31**

Scale, **22**
Shrew, Common, **25**
Slug, Black, **24**
Spider, **27**
Spruce, Norway, **5, 8, 10, 12, 16, 24, 28**; Sitka, **3**
Squirrel, Red, **24**
Sycamore, **4, 5, 6, 7, 11, 18, 31**

Tent caterpillar, **22**
Timberman, **24**
Tit, Blue, **25**
Toad, Common, **25**
Tortrix, Green, **22**

Treecreeper, **24**
Tulip Tree, **5, 31**

Walnut, **11, 17, 31**
Weevil, Nut, **22**; Pine, **22**
White Pine Blister Rust, **22**
Whitebeam, **11, 30**
Willow, **11, 17**; Crack, **8, 15**; Goat or Pussy, **29**; Weeping, **4, 12, 29**
Wood Anemone, **25**
Wood Louse, **27**
Woodpecker, Green, **25**; Great Spotted, **24**

Yew, **4, 16, 28**

Books to Read

A Field Guide to the Trees of Britain and Northern Europe. Alan Mitchell (Collins)
The Oxford Book of Trees. A. R. Clapham and B. E. Nicholson (Oxford)
Know Your Broadleaves and *Know Your Conifers.* H. L. Edlin (H.M.S.O.)
British Trees in Colour. Cyril Hart and Charles Raymond (Michael Joseph)
Trees and Bushes in Wood and Hedgerow. H. Vedel & J. Lange (Eyre Methuen)
The *Observer's Book of Trees.* W. J. Stokoe (Warne)
The World of a Tree. Arnold Darlington (Faber and Faber)
Woodland Life. G. Mandahl-Barth (Blandford)

Clubs and Societies

The Council for Environmental Conservation (address: Zoological Gardens, Regent's Park, London NW1) will supply the addresses of your local **Natural History Societies.** (Send a stamped self-addressed envelope for the list.) Many of these have specialist sections and almost all have field meetings. **The Royal Society for Nature Conservation** (address: 22 The Green, Nettleham, Lincoln) will give you the address of your local **County Naturalist Trust,** which may have a junior branch. Many of the Trusts have meetings and lectures and offer opportunities for work on nature reserves.
The Woodland Trust, Westgate, Grantham, Lincs, NG31 6LL.

The Royal Forestry Society of England, Wales and Northern Ireland, 102 High Street, Tring, Herts.
The Royal Scottish Forestry Society, 18 Abercromby Place, Edinburgh EH3 6LB.
The Arboricultural Association, 59 Blythwood Gardens, Stansted, Essex.
The Council for the Protection of Rural England, 4 Hobart Place, London SW1 will send you a leaflet on *Making a Tree Survey* as well as other leaflets and posters. Leaflets and information can also be obtained from **The Forestry Commission,** Information Branch, 235 Corstorphine Road, Edinburgh, EH12 7AT.

PRINTED IN BELGIUM